Lazy Sloth

Written by Jill Eggleton

Illustrated by Fraser Williamson

Rigby

The animals in the book

Sloth

Monkey

Monkey's friends

The tree in the book

A sloth lives in a tree. It goes upside down. It stays upside down for days and days. It is very slow.

Monkey saw Sloth upside down in a tree.

"**What are you doing?**" said Monkey.

Sloth didn't move.

"**Can you hear me?**"
shouted Monkey.

But Sloth's eyes stayed shut.

The next day,
Monkey came back.
Sloth was still in the tree.

"Are you OK?"
shouted Monkey.
"Can I help you get down?"

But Sloth didn't move, and
his eyes stayed shut.

Monkey got Parrot.

"Look at Sloth," he said. "He has been in the tree for days, and his eyes are shut!"

Parrot went...

TAP, TAP, TAP

with his beak on Sloth's claws. Sloth didn't move.

"He's sick," said Parrot.

Monkey looked at Sloth.

"Poor Sloth," he said.
"He must have a bed."

"Tiger can make one," said Parrot.

Parrot went to see Tiger.

"Sloth is sick," he said.
"Can you make a bed for him?"

Tiger will...

make a bed?

go away?

So Tiger made a hole
in the ground for a bed.
He put in leaves
to keep Sloth warm.
Monkey looked at the bed.

"Sloth's big," he said.
"You'll have to make
the bed bigger."

Tiger worked all day.

Monkey and Parrot shouted,
"Bigger,
bigger,
bigger!"

Tiger made the bed
ENORMOUS!
He was very tired.

"That's it," said Tiger.
"Now go and get Sloth."

"Sloth is very big," said Monkey.
"We'll have to get Elephant."

Elephant will...

get Sloth down?

go away?

Parrot and Monkey
went to get Elephant.

"Sloth is sick," said Parrot.
"He hasn't moved
for days and days.
Can you help us
get him into bed?"

"Where is he?" said Elephant.

"He's over there," said Monkey.

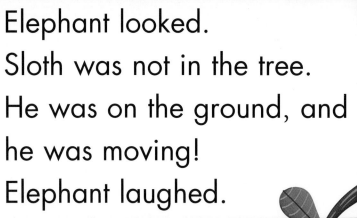

Elephant looked.
Sloth was not in the tree.
He was on the ground, and he was moving!
Elephant laughed.

"He's not sick," Elephant said.
"He's just lazy.
That's what sloths are!"

Monkey and Parrot were mad, but Tiger was **very** mad!

Tiger shouted,
"I made Sloth this big bed.
What are we going
to do with it now?"

"We'll have a party in it,"
said Parrot.

Party!

Yeah!

Party!

So the animals had a party.
But Sloth didn't come.
He was back in the tree!
His eyes were shut and
he wasn't moving.

That lazy, lazy sloth!

The End

Story sequence

Did the story go like this?

Did the story go like this?

Word Bank

beak

claws

leaves

ground